Contents

Rating FATHERS

Analyse the cover design and illustration and make a prediction about the target audience.

Predict

"My pappy could wup your pappy any day of the week, Josh Barrow!"

I looked at my friend Ben Goodnight and said nothing. What was there to say?
His pappy could wup my pappy any day of the week.
No argument.

Old man Goodnight was a huge bear of a man – all belly and shoulders. He owned the Goodnight Saloon in town.
He and Ben lived in a couple of small rooms out the back.
Ben didn't have a ma. She left when he was just a little boy.

On Friday and Saturday nights, Mr Goodnight tended bar, and every Sunday Ben would boast of the hardcases his pa had beaten up.

Clarify
wup
hardcases
dished out
sassing

... with bodies and BROKEN furniture FLYING through THE AIR

One time, three drunken cowboys had tried their luck against Mr Goodnight. When the dust had settled, Mr Goodnight was still standing and those three cowboys had to be carried out on stretchers.

I loved that story – especially the way Ben told it, with bodies and broken furniture flying through the air.

There wasn't a Sunday went by without Ben telling me of the beating his father had dished out the night before. Sometimes Ben would be sporting a few bruises and a black eye himself. For sassing his pa, he said.

I know my pa didn't cotton to a grown man using his fists on his own son, but then Pa didn't really cotton to a man using his fists any time, so I didn't pay him much heed.

You see, I'd never known Pa to get into a fight.

Not once. I don't know why, because he was a big man. Not like Mr Goodnight, but he was still tall and years of working on the land had made him solid.

All the other boys at school, their fathers had got into a fight at least once. One had even been in a gun battle with Indians way out west. But not my pa. And I don't mind telling you it made me feel ashamed.

So, when Ben told me his pa could wup mine, I'd just keep my mouth shut and quietly fume inside.

What else could I do? Sometimes I'd feel like taking a swipe at Ben, but he took after his father in size and temperament and I knew he'd make me eat dirt.

Colloquialism/Slang/Metaphor
What literary devices has the author used here? How did it help your understanding?

Language Features

Reading Between the Lines
Why do you think Josh, the narrator, felt ashamed of his pa? What factors influence his opinion?

Life on a DIRT FARM

We were farmers. Well, Pa was. I just sort of helped out with the chores between going to school and doing my studies. That was another thing about Pa. Always going on about how important it was for me to learn my letters and numbers. *He didn't mind that I didn't help out around the place as much as other boys helped their folks.* Just so long as I kept up my learning. That suited me down to the ground.

Clarify
lumberjacks

Our farm was in the state of Minnesota, about ten miles outside the town of Northfield.

It wasn't anything special as farms go. Twenty acres of cattle and crops. We lived in a four-room, single-storey weatherboard house that the wind whistled through. It came with the farm when my pa bought it ten years ago, when I was only three. There was a barn and an outhouse and a coop full of chickens.

Nothing MUCH happened IN NORTHFIELD...

Besides what we earned from the farm, Ma made dresses and such for the womenfolk in Northfield, so we got by okay.

Like our farm, Northfield wasn't much of a place. Just a few streets of dirt and horse dung, but it did have an iron bridge spanning the Cannon River that cut through the middle of town. That was kind of special.

Nothing much happened in Northfield, except on Saturday nights when cowboys and lumberjacks came into town to drink away their pay.

How effectively have the author, illustrator and designer developed the setting? Is the historical context credible? Why/why not?

Setting

What can you infer so far about the type of man Josh's father is?

Character Analysis

The DUSTERS

Every Saturday afternoon, Pa and I took the wagon into town to get our weekly supplies from the Lee Hitchcock Merchandise Store. *That particular Saturday started out just like all the others.* But what was about to happen would etch that date on my mind forever. September 7, 1876.

It was coming up to two in the afternoon when we trundled across the iron bridge and into the main town square where the store and just about every other building of importance was located. Across the way was the First National Bank, with its red brick walls and big windows. And right next to the store was the Goodnight Saloon.

Ben was sitting outside, just like he always did on a Saturday, and his face lit up at our approach.

Question

Why do you think Josh realised only in later years that "just about everyone, adult and child alike, treated my pa with respect"?

"Hey, Mr Barrow, you stopping off for a beer today?"

Sometimes, after we'd loaded up the wagon, Pa would go into the saloon for a drink and Ben and I would sit on the sidewalk and sip the soda pops Pa had bought us and figure out what we'd do the next day after church.

"Sorry, Ben, but we're running kind of late today," Pa replied. Ben's face fell. "Tell you what, though," Pa went on. "How about I buy you boys a soda pop anyway and you can drink it while I get the supplies."

Ben beamed. "Yessir, Mr Barrow! Thank you kindly!"

I always thought it strange that, even though Ben would tease me about how his father could wup mine, whenever he was face to face with Pa he'd be as respectful as anything. Thinking back now, I realise that just about everyone, adult and child alike, treated my pa with respect.

We hitched up the wagon and Pa brought us our soda pops and we sat near the sidewalk and started making plans.

Clarify

shiver of fear
outfit
jabbering

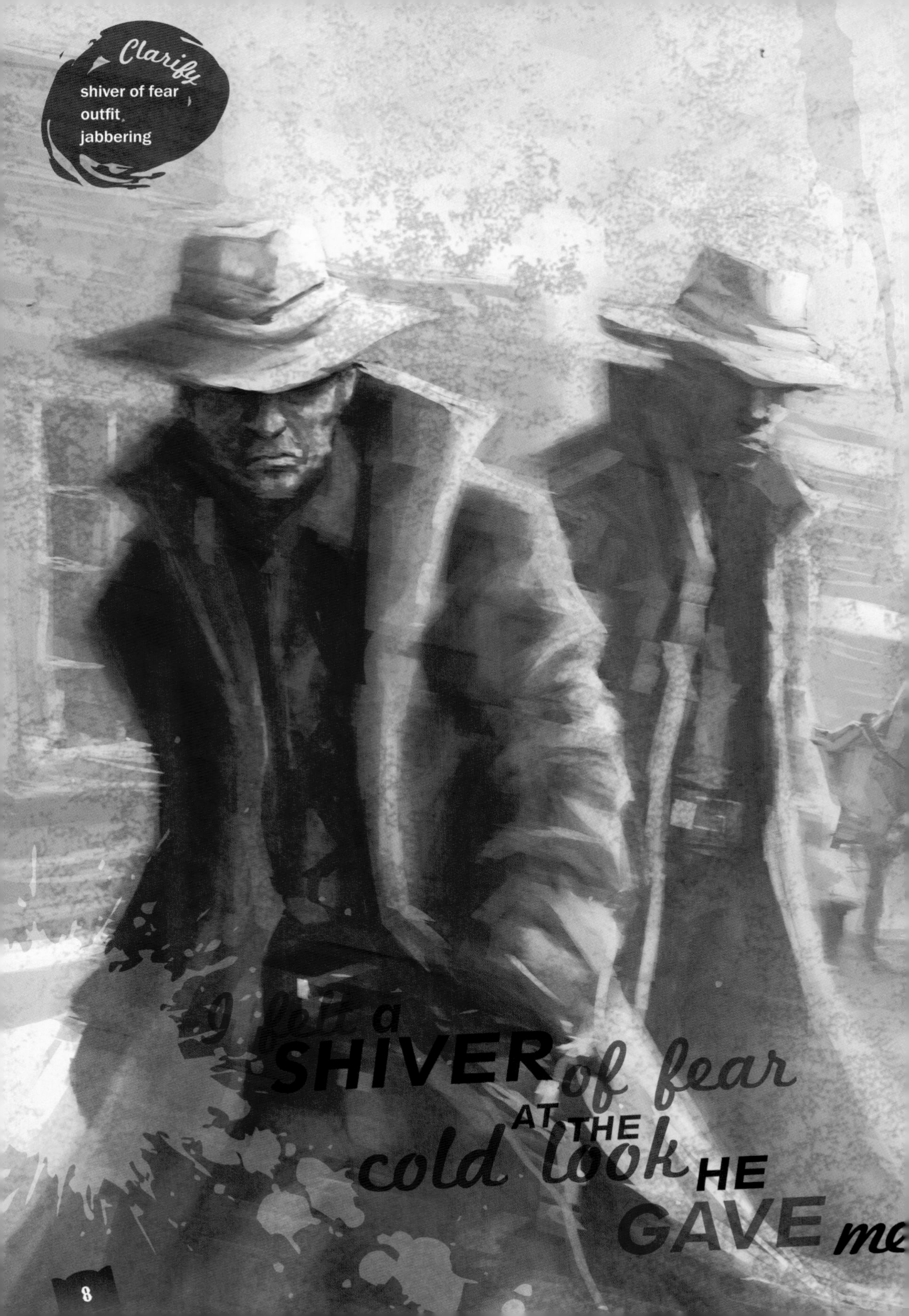

That's when I noticed a couple of strangers tying their horses to the hitching rail directly outside the saloon. They were dressed in long pale coats that reached down below their knees. *Dusters, the cattlemen called them.* I figured they were cowboys starting their drinking early.

What do you think will happen in the storyline now?

Plot

One of them met my eye and I don't mind admitting I felt a shiver of fear at the cold look he gave me. I waited for them to go into the bar, but they just folded their arms and stood there, surveying the street.

"Yo ho!"

It was August Soborn, one of the boys from school. He was a bit older than Ben and me, and he was Swedish or some such thing and couldn't speak a lick of American. But he was a good fellow and we got on fine.

He strode across the street towards us, pausing to make way for a half-dozen riders. They wore dusters, too. Must be part of the same outfit, I thought. Mr Goodnight would have his hands full tonight once these boys were through drinking.

But then they turned towards the First National and I figured they were going to bank their wages instead of trading them in for whiskey and beer. *Three of them stayed mounted while the others trooped inside.*

That struck me as kind of strange, but I didn't have time to dwell on it as August had reached us by now and was jabbering away in that funny language of his. Ben and I just smiled and nodded now and then and that seemed to keep August happy. Then his eyes fell on the horses outside the saloon – the ones the two cowboys had ridden up on. If there's one thing August admired, it was horseflesh.

Do you think the term "funny language" is a fair or biased description of a foreign language? Why?

Opinion

Beyond the Text
Do you think language difficulties are a barrier to making friends? Why/why not? What connections can you make to this?

Tipping his hat, August took his leave of us and approached the strangers. *I wanted to stop him. There was something about those two men that didn't sit right*. But it was too late by then. August was already there, patting the horses and chatting away to their owners. One of them just stared at him. The surly one turned his back and ignored him.

The bell over the store door tinkled and Pa came out with an armful of supplies. Old man Hitchcock followed him, equally laden.

I gulped down the last of my soda pop and helped load the wagon. We'd just finished tying everything down when Pa slapped his forehead with the flat of his hand.

"I forgot your ma's calico." He smiled at me.
"If I don't get it, she'll skin me. Won't be long."

Clarify

sit right
surly
calico
averted

But it was TOO late BY then

Do you think Josh should have been more proactive and warned August that he had bad feelings about the men outside the saloon? Why/why not?

Opinion

He ruffled my hair and disappeared back into the store. I watched him go and, as I did, I caught the eye of that surly cowboy again. I quickly averted my gaze.

I often wonder how things would have turned out if Pa hadn't gone back into the store. If we'd left town just a few minutes earlier.

Pa reappeared with a large brown paper parcel wrapped up tight with string.

"Time to go, Josh." He nodded at Ben.
"Guess we'll be seeing you tomorrow, Ben?"
"Yes, sir, Mr Barrow."

Analyse

What relevance does the illustration depicting the communication between the horse and August have to the story? What underlying message does this image convey?

11

Jesse JAMES!

Clarify
hollering
thwarted
posses

I cast a worried look over at August. He'd stopped talking now and was stroking one of the horses, a broad smile on his wide, flat face.

The surly cowboy was glaring at him. And then he gave him a shove. *"Get out of here, you crazy Dutchman,"* he growled.

I was the only one who saw it. I wanted to yell out that August didn't mean any harm and to stop pushing him around like that, but then the doors of the bank flew open and Mr Haywood, one of the cashiers, came out, waving his arms and hollering at the top of his voice.

"Jesse James is robbing the bank! Jesse James is robbing the bank!"

Jesse James! There wasn't a boy in town who hadn't heard of Jesse James and how he and his brother Frank and their gang robbed banks and railroads in daring raids and thwarted the bungling efforts of posses and the Pinkerton detective agency to catch them.

They were braver than Robin Hood and smart with it. We figured those wealthy folks who owned the railroads and the banks could probably afford to have a bit of money going astray, so Jesse and his boys weren't really doing anyone any harm.

Issue

Prejudice – opinion based on little knowledge, irrational feelings and stereotype
Find an example of prejudice. What effect does prejudice have on its victims and on influencing opinions of others in society? What connections can you make to this issue?

And now they were here, robbing our bank. And I was going to see it all.

"We figured those wealthy folks… could probably afford to have a bit of money going astray, so Jesse and his boys weren't really doing anyone any harm." What is your stance on Josh's "approval" of the robbing of the rich?

Jesse and **HIS BOYS** *weren't* **REALLY** **DOING** *anyone* **ANY HARM**

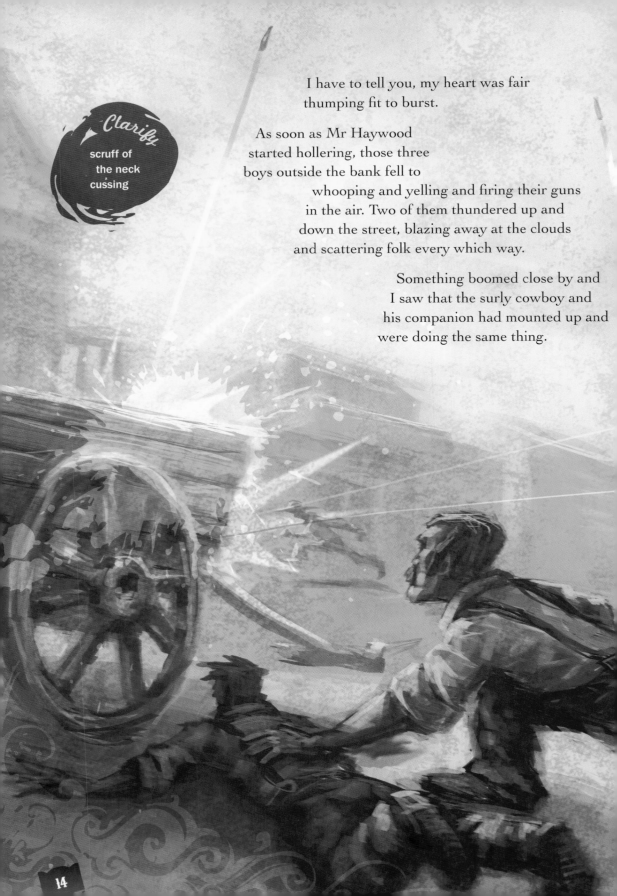

Clarify

scruff of
the neck
cussing

I have to tell you, my heart was fair
thumping fit to burst.

As soon as Mr Haywood
started hollering, those three
boys outside the bank fell to
whooping and yelling and firing their guns
in the air. Two of them thundered up and
down the street, blazing away at the clouds
and scattering folk every which way.

Something boomed close by and
I saw that the surly cowboy and
his companion had mounted up and
were doing the same thing.

A bee whizzed OVERHEAD and shattered THE window DIRECTLY behind HIM

How does the author's use of language evoke the world of Jesse James?

Language Features

Next thing, Pa had me by the scruff of the neck and pulled me down on the dirt behind the wagon.

"Stay down!" he hissed, and I felt his hand push into my back, so I didn't have any choice in the matter.

Ben was yahooing and capering around on the sidewalk just behind us. *"Hooo wheeee! Go get 'em, boys!"* he was yelling.

A bee whizzed overhead and shattered the window directly behind him. He didn't even notice, he was so caught up in it all.

"Dammit! Stay put!" And then Pa was up and grabbing Ben and dragging him back to our spot behind the wagon. Ben was struggling and cussing fit to turn the air blue, but Pa just pushed us both flat and lay over the top of us so we couldn't budge.

Even so, I still managed to get a good view of things between the legs of our bucking horses.

Analyse

Why do you think Ben failed to recognise the danger he was in when the shooting started?

15

The outlaw who'd stayed put outside the bank shouted, "Jesse, come on!" and there he was, large as life, standing at the door with a gun in one hand and a saddlebag in the other. *Jesse James.*

He looked around, calm as you please, as the bullets flew thick in the air and I remember thinking that he didn't look too much different from any other man.

Clarify

oath
batwing doors

He leaped onto his horse and called out to his brother Frank, and that's when I saw the second of the James boys, though he had his hat pulled down tight so I didn't get a good look at his face.

I heard an oath behind me. Mr Goodnight came thundering through the batwing doors of his saloon. He had a rifle and he put it to his shoulder and shot that surly cowboy clean out of his saddle. I figure the cowboy was dead before he hit the ground, but as he fell the pistol in his hand went off *and I saw poor old August Soborn drop like a stone.*

It stopped being fun after that.

It was screaming and shooting and dying. The outlaws weren't firing into the air any more. They were shooting for real. And the townsfolk were blazing back from windows and doors.

One of the outlaws was lying out in the street, his pale coat splashed with dirt and blood. And there was Mr Haywood, face down and arms outstretched. As I watched, another of the gang tumbled from his mount. He got up quick-smart and hobbled over to the shelter of a staircase alongside the building opposite.

Metaphor/Simile/Personification
What literary devices has the author used here? How did it help your understanding?

Language Features

16

"It stopped being fun after that." What inference can you make from this statement?

Inference

...and there HE WAS, large AS LIFE, STANDING AT the door WITH A gun....

Beyond the Text

Do you think violence in electronic media today creates insensitivity to real-life violence? Why/why not? What connections can you make to this?

Issue

What is your stance on the issue of guns in the community? Do you think laws regulating the sale of guns are necessary? Why/why not?

Frank James thundered by, his leg red and wet. Most of the gang had given up shooting by now. They were just looking for a way out.

"We're beat, boys!" Jesse yelled. He wheeled his horse and galloped off. Frank and the others lit out after him.

"Hold on! Don't leave me! I'm shot!"

It was the one who'd gone to ground beneath the stairway. He hobbled out onto the street, sobbing and waving his arms.

Clarify

lit out
ventured

18

I thought he was a goner for sure, and then one of the outlaws rode back through the storm of bullets and hauled him up onto his horse. A bullet picked his hat right off his head, but that didn't slow him down any.

Oxymoron/Metaphor/Simile/ Personification/Alliteration
What literary devices has the author used here? How did it help your understanding?

Language Features

The silence was *deafening*.

Townsfolk slowly ventured out onto the street and milled about among the bodies. No one was saying anything. It was as if they couldn't believe what had just happened.

I found myself drawn over to my friend August Soborn.

He lay there on his back, blue eyes staring sightlessly up at the sky.

I vomited.

No one was SAYING anything

"He lay there on his back, blue eyes staring sightlessly up at the sky."
What feelings are evoked when the author describes August's dead body in the street? How does this influence your feelings about violence? Can you relate to Josh's response?

Personal Response

Outlaws OUTSIDE the DOOR

Clarify

brooked no
argument
britches

It was getting towards dusk when we got back home. Ma appeared at the doorway as we unhitched the horses and settled them into the barn for the night. By the time we brushed them down and fed them, it was almost dark. *We hadn't spoken a word since leaving town.*

We came out into the chill evening air and that's when we saw the two riders appear from the gloom. I recognised the pale dusters immediately.

"Get inside with your ma, Josh," Pa said in a tone that brooked no argument.

I retreated into the house, my heart thumping, and Pa strode across the yard to face the riders.

Ma and I found a place by the window where we could watch. My breath fogged up the glass, so I had to keep wiping at it with my sleeve.

Pa stood in the middle of the yard, his feet slightly apart, hands by his side. He stood tall and straight and didn't even flinch when the riders reined up just a few feet in front of him.

You shot down LAW-ABIDING *folk, INCLUDING* A BOY BARELY *out of his* BRITCHES

The evening was still. The birds had stopped squawking with the setting of the sun. I could hear everything that was said, crystal clear.

My pa started it.

"You're not welcome here, Jesse James."

Old Jesse sure looked pleased that my pa knew who he was.

"You heard of me," he said with a grin.

"I saw what you did in town." My pa's voice was icy, like when he's caught me doing something I shouldn't.

Jesse's face darkened with that. "You one of the peckerwoods that shot my boys all to hell?"

"No. But I'd be lying if I said you boys didn't get what you deserved. You shot down law-abiding folk, including a boy barely out of his britches."

"We're not proud of that, mister." Frank James had spoken at last. For the first time, I took a good look at him. But, if you ask me now what he looked like, all I could tell you was that he had big ears. They stuck out of the side of his head like the wings of a bird. He shifted uncomfortably in his saddle, his pants stiff with dried blood. "But I reckon that boy would still be alive if that fat man hadn't come out of the saloon blasting away with that rifle of his."

Symbolism

"[Pa] stood tall and straight and didn't even flinch when the riders reined up just a few feet in front of him." What is symbolic about Pa's body language? What connections can you make to the underlying meaning?

Do you think the author has stereotyped the outlaws? Why/why not?

Opinion

21

A silence fell on the yard as they all thought about that.

Frank spoke again. "We need to hole up for the night. Then we'll be on our way."

▶ Clarify

hole up

He said it as if Pa would just roll over and say sure, but my pa would have none of it.

"You are murderers and thieves. You are not welcome here."

That's when Jesse pulled his gun. It was a big, black, ugly thing.

I felt my mother's fingers dig into my shoulders, so hard that it hurt. My breath caught in my throat and there was a funny ringing in my ears. I watched, frozen, as Jesse pointed that pistol right at my pa's head.

I had to do something! But my legs wouldn't move. I just stood there at the window and watched. It was as if one of those stories I'd read about Jesse James had sprung to life and it wasn't my pa out there looking down the barrel of a gun, but some stranger.

"Maybe I'll just blow your brains out and we'll stay here anyway," Jesse was saying.

My pa still didn't move. He was probably as scared as I was. Rooted to the spot. But then he spoke, and there was no trace of fear in his voice.

Reading Between the Lines

Why do you think Josh has trouble differentiating between the real-world events in his yard and the storybook world of Jesse James? What parallels can you draw?

"You fire that hand cannon of yours, Jesse James, and you'll bring in every sheriff and deputy who's hunting for you."

That got the two outlaws looking around. Then Jesse turned back, his face all twisted up and ugly with a sneer. "I don't have to shoot you. I can just get off my horse and treat you to a pistol whipping. What do you say to that?"

Question Generate

What questions can you ask about the way myths create heroes such as Jesse James?

"You can try," my pa replied, without even a pause.

Pa had his back to me, so I couldn't see the expression on his face. But Jesse could see it as plain as day and what he saw made that sneer disappear from his face. After what seemed an age, he shoved his pistol back in his holster.

"The hell with you, old man," he snorted.

"You're not worth it."

He pulled cruelly on his reins and he and Frank turned and started to ride off into the gloom.

They were leaving. And Pa was letting them go! It wasn't right. Not after all they'd done.

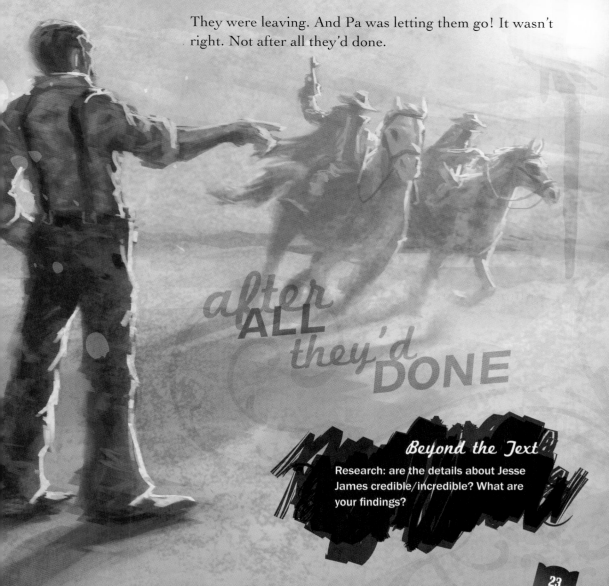

after ALL they'd DONE

Beyond the Text

Research: are the details about Jesse James credible/incredible? What are your findings?

Settling of SCORES

Before my ma could stop me, I had snatched the hunting rifle from the wall and burst out into the yard. I saw Pa looking at me with wide eyes. I wasn't even thinking but, before I could lift the barrel of that big, heavy gun, I pulled the trigger.

The click of the empty chamber sounded sharp and loud in the still night air.

Jesse heard it and whirled. The expression I saw on his face froze my blood.

What analogy did the author use here? What did he want to convey to the reader?

Analogy

Clarify

chamber
heavy silence

...I wasn't EVEN THINKING...
I knew THAT I WAS dead

It wasn't the face of a normal man. He looked like one of those wild critters that Ben and I would corner sometimes – all snarling and fury. He pulled his pistol in one fast, fluid motion and pointed it right at me. The whole world seemed to be swallowed up by that huge black barrel and I knew that I was dead.

And then Pa was between us, his arms outstretched, blocking me from Jesse's line of fire.

"He's only a boy," Pa said. "How many more boys do you want to kill today, Jesse James?"

At any moment I expected to hear the boom of Jesse's pistol. But there was nothing. Only a heavy silence that stretched on and on.

"Come on, Jesse," Frank said at last.

I heard Jesse laugh. It wasn't a nice thing to hear. "Your boy's got more grit than you do, mister."

And then they were gone.

Pa stood there, watching them go, until the drumming hooves faded into silence. He turned and looked me right in the eye. I felt the rifle, empty and useless, slip from my fingers.

Pa raised his arms and for a moment I thought he was going to hit me. But, the next thing I knew, he had those big strong arms of his wrapped around me and he was hugging me close and tight. I felt his tears wet on my cheek and that started me to crying. I heard Ma race out of the house and then she was wrapping us both up in her arms and we all stood there, blubbering like babies.

What is meant by "heavy silence"?

Imagery

Beyond the Text

"The whole world seemed to be swallowed up by that huge black barrel and I knew that I was dead." What images does the text create for you? Can you relate to Josh and the fear he experiences?

I changed that night. It wasn't that I noticed anything different right off. But Ben and I didn't see too much of each other after that. His stories about his pa wupping drunks didn't seem to matter to me any more.

I guess he sensed it and, after a while, he stopped coming around.

Five years later, old man Goodnight wupped one drunk too many. The next morning, the cowboy came back into the saloon and shot Ben's pa while he was eating a plateful of fried eggs.

Ben was **long gone** by then. On his sixteenth birthday, he up and left without a word. Just like his ma did all those years ago. No one knew where he went, not even his pa. But I take comfort in the thought that he's surely better off where he is now than where he was before.

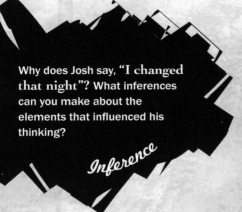

Why does Josh say, "I changed that night"? What inferences can you make about the elements that influenced his thinking?

Inference

Jesse James died bloody, too. I heard his own gang shot him while he was straightening a picture in his parlour.

They had to shoot him in the back, though. Not like my pa.

He faced down Jesse James and didn't even have a gun.

What inferences can you make about
Ben's early life with his father and the
reasons he left town?

Character Analysis

Jesse JAMES *died* BLOODY, TOO

Why do you think the author
wrote this story? What message
does he want to convey to the
reader?

Author Purpose

Think about THE TEXT

Making Connections

What connections can you make to the characters, plot, setting and themes of *Facing Jesse James?*

Being powerless

Dealing with violence

Dealing with the death of a friend

Being afraid for family

Dealing with bullying

Text to SELF

Feeling compassion

Feeling ashamed

Facing social prejudice

Changing your opinion

Facing consequences

Making rash decisions

Text to TEXT/MEDIA

Talk about texts/media you have read, listened to or seen that have similar themes and compare the treatment of theme and the differing author styles.

Text to WORLD

Talk about situations in the world that might connect to elements in the story.

Planning an HISTORICAL FICTION

1 Think about what defines historical fiction

Historical fiction connects the reader with the situations and events of history. It incorporates an historical period and historical events as a background for the thoughts and actions of characters – fictitious or real.

2 Think about the plot

Decide on a plot that has an introduction, problems and a solution, and write them in the order of sequence.

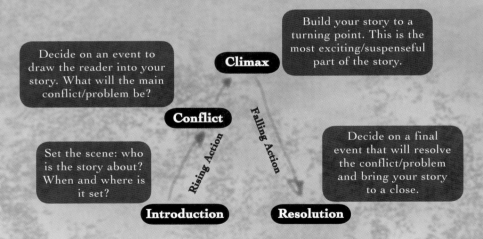

Build your story to a turning point. This is the most exciting/suspenseful part of the story.

Climax

Decide on an event to draw the reader into your story. What will the main conflict/problem be?

Conflict

Falling Action

Rising Action

Set the scene: who is the story about? When and where is it set?

Decide on a final event that will resolve the conflict/problem and bring your story to a close.

Introduction

Resolution

Think about the sequence of events and how to present them using researched knowledge of the historical time frame.

Think about
the characters

Explore:

- how characters from the chosen historical time frame think, feel and act

- what motivates their behaviour

- the social structures that affect their status and behaviour.

Decide on
the setting

Atmosphere/mood ⟶ location ⟶ time

Think about the setting and how to present it using researched knowledge of the historical time frame.

> *Note:* Historical fiction is usually set in one period of time or explores one aspect of history.

Writing an HISTORICAL FICTION

Have you. . .

- Made links to the society and events of your period?

- Maintained historical accuracy about actual events or settings?

- Been true to the context of your time frame?

- Provided a window on the past?

- Explored values and beliefs of the time?

- Developed characters that will stand up to in-depth analysis?

...don't forget to revisit your writing.

Do you need to change, add or delete anything to improve your story?